JEFFREY AND
THE THIRD-GRADE GHOST
Max Saves the Day

Other Jeffrey and the Third-Grade Ghost Books
#1 Mysterious Max
#2 Haunted Halloween
#3 Christmas Visitors
#4 Pet Day Surprise
#5 Max Onstage

Jeffrey and the Third-Grade Ghost

BOOK SIX

Max Saves the Day

Megan Stine
AND
H. William Stine

FAWCETT COLUMBINE
NEW YORK

Chapter One

The way Jeffrey Becker was racing and rushing around his bedroom meant that it had to be a Saturday morning. On Saturdays, Jeffrey always hurried to get out of the house in twelve and a half minutes flat. On this particular Saturday morning, though, Jeffrey was six minutes into his wake-up routine when he hit a problem.

When he opened the top drawer of his bedroom dresser to grab a pair of socks, he saw only one red sock, one blue, one white, one white with green stripes, and one white with blue spots—from stepping on blueberries. "Hey!" Jeffrey said out loud. "Nothing matches!"

Then he opened the second drawer. Everything looked normal, so he took his hairbrush out and began to brush his thick brown hair. But after only a couple of strokes, he looked as if he had just stepped out of a snowstorm. There was talcum powder buried in the bristles of his hairbrush.

The missing socks and the hairbrush were a

mystery—for about five seconds. "Okay, where are you, Max?" Jeffrey asked, looking around his empty room.

The room may have looked empty, but it wasn't. There was a ghost in it somewhere, and Jeffrey knew it.

"Max," Jeffrey said, calling the ghost's name again. "I know you're here. Stop making yourself invisible."

"Hey, Daddy-o. Like, what big dandruff you have," a voice in the room said suddenly. And slowly Max appeared, floating up near the ceiling. Max was a third-grader, just like Jeffrey. But he didn't look or sound like any of Jeffrey's other friends. With his baggy jeans, his white T-shirt with the sleeves rolled up almost to his shoulders, and his hair greased back, Max looked like a kid from the 1950s. And that's because he was one!

"Never fear, Max is here," the ghost said. "Start shakin' and movin' cause this cat is groovin'."

Jeffrey rolled his eyes and laughed. "Most people just say hi. What's with the poetry?"

"Don't be cruel. It isn't cool," the ghost answered. "Besides, I'm in a rhyming mood today. It's hipper than hip."

Jeffrey grabbed his baseball glove. It was an old glove that Max had given him. "Let's go," Jeffrey said.

"Like, where?"

"Where do you think?" Jeffrey answered. "You said we'd play some baseball today."

"Like, that's what I fell by to tell you, Daddy-o," said the ghost. "I can't make the scene. Like, sorry, cat."

"Max," Jeffrey said, "you've canceled three weeks in a row. You said this time for sure."

"Like, did I say 'I promise'?"

Jeffrey nodded.

"Did I say 'I promise,' did I cross my heart and hope to die, kiss my pinkie, and spin around three times?"

Jeffrey nodded again.

"Like, did I say 'I promise,' cross my heart and hope to die, kiss my pinkie, spin around three times, walk like a duck, and stand on my head?"

"Well, no," Jeffrey admitted.

"Then, like, it doesn't count as a real promise, Daddy-o. Aren't you hip to how things are supposed to work?"

"Nothing works the way it's supposed to when you're around, Max," Jeffrey said with a sigh.

3

The ghost smiled. "You're just saying that because you dig me the most," he said, punching Jeffrey's arm lightly. "Like, next Saturday for absolutely sure, Daddy-o."

"Never mind," Jeffrey said. "I'm going to the park without you. I have lots of other friends who'll play ball with me."

But when Jeffrey got to the park on his bike, there was only one kid in sight: Brian Carr. And Brian was one of Jeffrey's least favorite people.

Brian Carr was down the hill by the playground. He's probably waiting around for someone to pick a fight with, Jeffrey thought. Brian was throwing rocks into a large mud puddle that looked almost big enough to swim across. Every rock splashed waves of muddy water all over the playground equipment.

As Jeffrey got closer, he saw that Arvin Pubbler was there, too. Arvin was trying to convince Brian to play baseball with him. "Come on, Brian. Let's play some baseball, huh, Brian? Baseball, huh, Brian? Baseball?"

"Arvin, you're a broken record," Brian said.

Arvin had a bad habit of always asking a question three times.

"Come on, Brian. Baseball, what do you say? Baseball, huh? Baseball?" Arvin repeated.

4

Just then, Brian stopped throwing large rocks into the large mud puddle—but only because he wanted to throw Arvin's baseball glove into it. Then Brian walked away. He didn't even look back.

Things like that always happened to Arvin Pubbler. Everyone, including Arvin, expected it. And usually everyone *except* Arvin laughed about it. But Jeffrey didn't laugh. He put his bike in the park bike rack and walked down the hill to Arvin.

Arvin gave Jeffrey a small wave. "Hi, Jeffrey." He stood staring at the mud puddle as if he hoped his baseball glove would magically learn to swim.

"I saw what Brian did," Jeffrey told him.

"Yeah," Arvin said sadly. "At least he didn't throw *me* in."

Arvin and Jeffrey searched the park for the longest tree branch they could find. Then, after many tries, Jeffrey finally hooked Arvin's dripping, muddy glove on the end of the branch and pulled it out of the mucky puddle.

"Thanks, Jeffrey," Arvin said. "Wanna play some baseball?"

"Uh, no thanks. Gotta go, Arvin," Jeffrey said. "My mom's calling me."

Jeffrey ran up the hill to get away from Arvin and to get his bike. But at the top, he stopped cold in his tracks. The bike rack was still there. The tree by the bike rack was still there. The metal trash can under the tree by the bike rack was still there. *But his bike was gone.*

"Great," he said to himself. "How could I have been so dumb that I forgot to lock my bike?" But then Jeffrey relaxed. He even smiled. "Max," he called. "Where are you? Bring back my bike!" He waited for the ghost to laugh or to show himself. But nothing happened.

Suddenly from behind him a voice yelled at Jeffrey. "Get out of the way, imbecile!"

Jeffrey turned around and jumped out of the

6

way just in time. A kid zipped past him on a bike. And he almost ran right into Jeffrey! The bike rider was someone Jeffrey had never seen before. He had curly bright red hair and was wearing white shorts and a green T-shirt. Where'd he come from? Who was he? For a second, Jeffrey didn't even notice the most important thing: The boy was riding *his* bike!

"Hey! That's my bike!" Jeffrey shouted.

The boy did a wheelie and stopped the bike about twenty feet from Jeffrey. "How do you know this is your bike?" he asked calmly. "I'll bet you don't even know what kind of a bike it is." As he talked, the red-haired boy spun a bike pedal with his foot.

"It's the kind that belongs to me," Jeffrey answered.

The boy shook his head and smiled. "Most bikes are either sport bikes or touring bikes. Sport bikes are lightweight and faster. Touring bikes are heavier and their longer frames absorb road bumps better. Which is this?"

"Read my lips," Jeffrey said. As he walked up to the boy, Jeffrey noticed that the name Robin was stitched in blue thread on his green T-shirt. "I didn't ask for an oral report on bicycles. I said, Get off mine!"

"You interrupted me. This is my point," the boy said. "Your bike represents a new category, a class by itself."

"Yeah? What?" Jeffrey asked coldly.

"It's a piece of junk."

The boy laughed, and Jeffrey jerked the handlebars, trying to grab the bike away. He hoped the boy would lose his balance and fall off. "If it's so crummy, why don't you just get off?" Jeffrey demanded.

"I'm not ready to, that's why," the red-haired boy said. "Can you do this?" He pulled away from Jeffrey. Then he leaned forward on the handlebars. With a quick jerk, he lifted the back wheel off the ground. For a minute, the bike did a perfect front wheelie.

"I haven't done that trick since I was two, but I probably still remember how," Jeffrey said quickly.

The boy smiled, but it was a mean smile. "You're lying," he said. "Sometimes lying means people are creative or have an independent spirit. Sometimes it just means they're complete jerks."

"Just get off my bike," Jeffrey said. "You can't steal it."

Jeffrey and the red-haired boy stared at each other. Their eyes didn't blink.

"I didn't *steal* your bike," the boy answered. "I'm just riding it. Stealing is taking and keeping property that doesn't belong to you. Do you know what petty theft is? It's when you steal something that costs less than five hundred dollars. Like this bike."

"What did you eat for breakfast? An encyclopedia?" Jeffrey asked. He'd never before met such a know-it-all.

The red-haired boy took off on the bike again. Jeffrey was about to chase him, when a familiar voice made him turn around.

"Hey, wow, Jeffrey, I thought you said you'd never let *anyone* ride your bike." It was Kenny Thompsen, one of Jeffrey's good friends. He was the only other person in the world who could see and hear Max.

"Kenny, I didn't *let* that geek ride my bike," Jeffrey snapped angrily. "He *stole* it."

"That's not right," Kenny said, shaking his head.

The two friends ran after the boy on the bike. But he was too fast for them. He rode the bike around the park, then zipped down the hill, bouncing toward the playground.

"Get off my bike!" Jeffrey shouted at the top of his voice.

"Whatever you say," answered the red-haired kid. Quickly he jumped off the bike. But, of course, the bike kept rolling until it came to a stop. *Splash!* It rolled right into the middle of the large mud puddle.

That did it. Jeffrey charged down the hill full-speed. He and the stranger glared at each other from opposite sides of the mud puddle.

"It's your fault. You told me to get off," the boy said. Then before Jeffrey could catch him, he ran away and disappeared over the hill.

For a minute, Jeffrey and Kenny just stared at the bike. One handlebar was the only thing sticking up out of the mud.

"Too bad Max wasn't here," Kenny said quietly to Jeffrey.

Jeffrey sighed. "Yeah, then we *really* would have been in trouble!"

Chapter Two

Jeffrey spent almost the entire weekend cleaning his bike, oiling the chain, and drying off the seat. It was hard work, but he stayed calm by imagining the horrible things he'd like to do to that know-it-all Robin. For one thing, he'd like to rubber cement his red hair and use him as an eraser. Or, worse yet, he'd make sure the kid was invited to Stephanie Pinchot's next birthday party. Stephanie's parents were into health foods, and their idea of a birthday cake was a solid brick of mashed sprouts. Their idea of a great party game was to pass around an avocado and feel its texture.

The new boy deserved to go to Stephanie's party—and more. In just five or six minutes, he had scored dozens of rat points, points Jeffrey gave people for being rotten. The boy had stolen his bike, made fun of him, refused to give the bike back, and then dropped it in a mud puddle. That was almost a perfect score.

But by Sunday night Jeffrey's shiny silver

bike was gleaming again. And Jeffrey went to bed willing to forget the whole thing. All he wanted was *never, ever* to see that kid again.

At school the next morning, the story about Jeffrey and the redheaded boy was all over the classroom—because Jeffrey was telling everyone about it.

"He tried to steal my bike, but I wouldn't let him. We had a big fight," Jeffrey said.

Melissa McKane, Jeffrey's next-door neighbor, raised her eyebrows, which were almost as red as her hair. "*You* got into a fight, Jeffrey?" she said teasingly. "I thought you said you could *talk* your way out of any fight."

"He came at me with a baseball bat," Jeffrey insisted.

Benjamin Hyde looked at Jeffrey over his gold wire-rimmed glasses. "You told me he came at you with a fork," he said.

"Ben, you're my best friend. I didn't want to scare you," Jeffrey said. "Anyway, I tried a couple of karate moves on him."

Ricky Reyes, who knew karate, was the toughest kid in the third grade. He was probably number two, if you counted the fourth grade, too. He looked at Jeffrey suspiciously. "Like what?" he said.

"Well, uh, I gave him a split-twist flying kick," Jeffrey said.

Ricky rolled his eyes. "Jeffrey, I told you that move is only good for opening my locker when the door's jammed."

"You *really* fought him, Jeffrey?" asked Melissa.

Jeffrey showed them the back of his left hand. "How do you think I got this scar?"

"I thought you said you got it last year when you saved a baby from a burning house," Ricky said.

"You told me it was from biting your fingernails too hard," Melissa said.

"You told me that an alien from outer space branded you to show that you were blood brothers," Ben said. "I like that story the best."

"I didn't mean *this* scar," Jeffrey grumbled. "I meant a scar I can't show you."

Kenny Thompsen walked into class just then, and their teacher, Mrs. Merrin, walked in right after him. Usually she sat on her desk to start the morning session. But not today. Today she stood at the door with one hand on the knob as she spoke to the class. "There's only four weeks of school left. Can you believe it? Not the time of year when we usually get a new student in class. But just the same, we are getting someone new today . . ."

Then she opened the classroom door and the redheaded boy from the park walked in! Jeffrey and Kenny practically slid out of their chairs in surprise.

Mrs. Merrin put her arm around the boy's shoulders, the way she always did when she really liked someone. "Class, this is Robin Dessart. He's a new student at Redwood Elementary School and I want you to make him feel at home. Robin, welcome to our class."

Robin didn't say anything or look at anyone. He just twisted his shoulders to squirm away from Mrs. Merrin. Finally she took her arm away.

"First," the teacher said, "let's go around the classroom and introduce ourselves to Robin."

"Don't bother," Robin said. "I have an excellent memory for faces." He was staring right at Jeffrey when he said it. He plopped down at an empty desk and scooted his chair away from Jenny Arthur as if bugs were jumping off her. "Can we do some work?" he asked. "That's what we're here for."

Behind Jeffrey, Ricky whispered, "Is he for real?"

Mrs. Merrin just smiled patiently and walked to the front of the class. She had changed out of her high heels and into a pair of red high-top sneakers for gym later that morning. "Robin," she said, nodding toward the chalkboard, "that's the Question of the Day. Anyone who knows the answer gets to be captain of one of the baseball teams in gym today."

Everyone read the question: Who is Sir Isaac Newton?

"Ben would know that," Jeffrey said, poking his best friend. Ben was smart about science. He wanted to be an inventor or a mad scientist when he grew up.

"Isaac Newton discovered gravity when an apple hit him on the head," said Ben.

"I thought a fig hit him on the head," Jeffrey joked. "Isn't that when he discovered the Fig Newton?"

Robin aimed a sneer at Ben and Jeffrey. "Don't you even know that Newton built the first reflecting telescope with a concave mirror?" he asked.

Ben sat silently, pushing his glasses up and down on his nose.

"Sure, Ben knew that," Jeffrey said quickly.

"He was telling me all about it when we walked to school this morning."

Robin just snorted and shook his head.

Later that morning in gym class, Robin earned some more rat points. It was during a baseball game. Melissa was playing right field; Robin was supposed to be playing center field. All of a sudden, Ricky Reyes smacked a hard fly ball straight toward Melissa. Melissa watched it without moving, but anyone who knew Melissa knew that she was ready to catch it.

But out of nowhere, Robin came charging over. "I've got it!" he shouted. "I've got it!" He ran right into Melissa and their legs got tangled. Melissa fell, but Robin kept running and yelling, "I've got it!"

By the time he caught the ball, Melissa was on her feet again. She grabbed his arm and yanked him around. "What's the big idea?" she demanded. "That ball was mine."

They were standing red head to red head, only Melissa's head was a little higher.

"It was a crucial out for our team. I had to make sure we caught the ball," Robin said.

Melissa's voice got softer, which was a sure sign that she was getting mad. "I have a brother who's a slimeball," she said. "He's in the fifth

16

grade. And even *he* knows better than to try to catch a ball in my territory. Get the picture?"

"Competition between brothers and sisters is

normal," Robin said confidently. "If you're having a problem with it, tell your parents, not me."

After school, Jeffrey, Melissa, Ben, Ricky, and Kenny walked home together.

"I hate Robin the most," Melissa said. "I've got two bruises on my leg where he ran into me."

"I hate him more than you do," Kenny said. "He told me that, statistically, short kids grow up to be short, poor adults who are always short of cash."

"I hate him for saying that to you," Ben said. "It's a lie, anyway."

"I hate him because Mrs. Merrin stood up for him all day," Jeffrey said. "When he said, 'Even a cat wouldn't eat the cafeteria food,' Mrs. Merrin didn't give him a detention. But she gave me one a few months ago when I said the same thing."

As they walked home, taking up most of the sidewalk, someone came up behind them and wanted to pass. It was Robin riding a unicycle. "Baa!" he shouted. "Look at the sheep."

"What's that supposed to mean?" snapped Melissa.

"The five of you look like a flock of sheep, the way you always stick together. Besides, sheep aren't very smart," Robin added. He looked pleased to have another opportunity to tell them something they didn't know. "In fact, they're so dumb that if one sheep jumps off a mountain, the other sheep just follow."

Ricky Reyes stopped and turned around with his hands on his hips. "Look, man, why don't you just get lost?" he said.

Robin's mouth opened in a big, long yawn.

"I don't like you," Ricky said.

"After you get to know me better, you'll really learn to hate me," Robin promised. He stepped off his unicycle. Then he and Ricky circled each other, moving closer and closer. Robin raised his hands karate-style. Jeffrey and his other friends moved back. They knew there was no way to tell Ricky Reyes to back off from a fight.

"My kung-fu instructor taught me the secrets of the silent cobra, an invincible army of Chinese tong warriors," Robin bragged.

"I can handle that," Ricky said. Fast as an eye blink, he kicked out at Robin, who was trying to punch him in the stomach. Then Ricky grabbed Robin's arm and flipped him backward onto the ground.

Suddenly, a car horn started blasting. Everyone looked toward the street. A small red car had pulled over, and the driver, Mrs. Merrin, was running toward the fight.

She helped Robin off the ground and glared at Ricky. "I don't even want to know what this is about or who started it," she said to Ricky and Jeffrey, who was standing nearby.

"We were just giving Robin a guided tour of the neighborhood," Jeffrey said, anyway. "This was the first stop: Mr. Fielding's front yard."

"I don't want any stories, Jeffrey," Mrs. Merrin said, putting a finger to her mouth. "I want apologies, especially from you, Ricky. I thought I made it clear in class that everyone should make Robin feel welcome. Now don't make me tell you again."

"Don't waste your breath," Robin said. He pulled away and rode off on his unicycle.

"Give him a chance, you guys," Mrs. Merrin said. "Especially *you*, Jeffrey."

Chapter Three

No one said a word—not even after Mrs. Merrin walked away, got into her car, then came back to tell everyone to have a good evening, got back into her car, and drove off.

"What's her problem?" Melissa asked at last, twisting her long red ponytail with her fingers. "Can't she see what a total pain Robin Dessart is?"

Ricky kicked the dirt in disgust. "All I know is, if Robin Dessart gets in my face again, I'm going to lay him out, for sure."

The five friends walked to the end of the street and then split up. Ben had to go home to take out the garbage—a chore he hated almost as much as he loved to complain about it. Melissa had a ballet lesson. And Ricky had a karate class.

That left Jeffrey and Kenny standing on the sidewalk. "You know what I was thinking when Ricky and Robin started to fight?" Kenny asked.

"Of course I know," Jeffrey said. "I can read

minds." He pressed his thumbs lightly against his forehead. "Go ahead and tell me. I'll see if I got it right."

"I was thinking that it was too bad Max wasn't here," Kenny said.

"That's exactly what I thought you were thinking."

Kenny looked at his friend skeptically. Kenny liked to believe everything everyone said, but Jeffrey really pushed it. "Anyway," Kenny said, "I wanted Max to be here because he would have stopped the fight."

"Max, stop a fight? He would have sold tickets," Jeffrey said with a laugh as he started to walk home.

"But Max is definitely on our side," Kenny insisted.

After taking a few more steps, Jeffrey stopped. He put his foot up on a fire hydrant to retie his sneaker. That's what he always did when he was getting an idea or thinking of a plan.

"You've got an idea?" Kenny asked. "Tell me."

"It's what you said," Jeffrey answered. "About Max. Maybe I can convince him to do something to Robin. But first I've got to *find* him."

The first place Jeffrey decided to look was the bowling alley. When he walked in, there was a big celebration going on. Everyone was cheering and pounding an old man on the back. But Max was nowhere around.

"Hi, Mr. Grindorf," Jeffrey said to the middle-aged man who ran the bowling alley and the snack bar. "What's going on?"

"Kid," Mr. Grindorf said, because that's what he called everything under the age of eighteen, including dogs. "Mr. McFurley just bowled a perfect game! He's ninety-two years old. He can't even lift a bowling ball without help. But every time he rolled the ball down the lane, he got a strike. Can you believe it?"

Jeffrey could believe it, all right. And he knew what it meant. Max had been here! Two of Max's favorite tricks were things he did in the bowling alley: number one was knocking down pins for people who were lousy bowlers. The other was holding the pins still—so they wouldn't fall down—when a show-off got up to bowl.

But Max was probably gone now. So Jeffrey hurried to the ice cream shop, another Max hangout.

As soon as he entered the Sweet Truth Ice Cream Shop, Jeffrey knew that Max had been

23

there, too. The tables, the chairs, the floors, and even the workers were covered with ice cream, whipped cream, and different flavored syrups.

"What happened?" Jeffrey asked the store manager.

"Someone put a sign in front of the store. It said, 'Hit someone in the face with an ice cream cone and get two cones absolutely freesville,'" explained the store manager, who had multicolored candy sprinkles stuck to her cheeks. "It was like a war."

Even though the trail was made of cool ice cream, it was getting hotter. Jeffrey ran to the grocery store next, hoping to catch Max in the act.

It was a large grocery store with many long, wide aisles. Jeffrey checked each aisle. Cutting through the cereal section, he ran past a mother who was busy scolding her daughter.

"Emily," said the mother to the three-year-old who sat in the shopping cart, "every time I turn my back, you put chocolate milk, chocolate cereal, or chocolate syrup in the shopping cart. I'm sick and tired of it."

"No, I didn't, Mommy," Emily whined.

The mother was angry. And her daughter didn't know what was going on. But Jeffrey did.

Max was grocery shopping again—putting things he liked into someone else's shopping cart!

"Excuse me, but it's not your daughter's fault," Jeffrey said to Emily's mother. "The store stacks all of the chocolate products so that they're easily tipped over. Just walking by them creates enough breeze so that they fall right into your cart."

Jeffrey wasn't sure the woman believed him, but she smiled and stopped blaming her daughter.

Jeffrey looked around, waiting for his ghostly friend to show up.

"Daddy-o!" Max suddenly appeared and

25

floated down from a stack of cereal boxes. "Like, what's the *small* idea? The fun was just starting."

"Where have you been, Max?"

"Aisle three," said the ghost. "They've got something new there called—dig this—fast foods. But, like, I've been eyeballing them for an hour and they still haven't moved. What's so fast about them?"

"That's not what we mean by fast foods, Max," Jeffrey said.

"Well, who doesn't know that?" Max looked away to hide his embarrassment. "You know, I invented fast foods."

"Of course," Jeffrey said, rolling his eyes. "You invented everything."

"Not everything, Daddy-o," said the ghost modestly. "Someone asked me to invent poison ivy, but, like, I didn't have the itch to do it. Ha ha ha ha!"

Max started walking down the aisle, still dropping cans of this and boxes of that into other people's carts. Finally, Jeffrey dragged him out of the store.

On the way home, Jeffrey told Max about Robin Dessart. Max listened, then said only one thing: "Glass-eye Willie Tufa."

"Glass-eye Willie Tufa?" Jeffrey repeated. "What is that? Another baseball player from the 1950s? Or is it a kind of fish?"

"He was a weirdsville cat at my school. He was such a square that he even blew square bubbles with bubble gum."

"Did he really have a glass eye?"

Max shook his head. "But, like, he was always saving his money to buy one—that's how weirdsville this cat was," the ghost explained. "Glass-eye and yours truly were like two trains heading toward each other on the same track. Just like you and Robin."

"Wow. What happened?"

Max looked at Jeffrey out of the corner of his eye. "On second thought, like, forget it. We need to groove to a different tune to take care of this cat, Robin," Max said.

"Wait a minute, Max," Jeffrey sputtered. "What happened between you and Glass-eye Willie Tufa?"

"Jeffrey, like, don't change the subject," Max said.

"Me?" Jeffrey protested. "*You* invented changing the subject. Right after you invented ducking the question."

"Cool it," Max said with a sly smile. "Genius

at work, Daddy-o. Can't you smell the rubber burning?"

By that time they were at Jeffrey's house. They sat on the front porch, although sometimes the ghost would fly around the house. He said his best ideas always came to him in the air.

"I know!" Max cried, hovering above Jeffrey's head. "And this is really groovy, Daddy-o. You want to make Robin think he's flipped his wig? When he makes the scene at schoolsville tomorrow, pretend that you can't understand a word he says."

"Max, is that what you did to Glass-eye Willie Tufa?" Jeffrey asked.

"Like, remind me to tell you some time," teased the ghost.

"I *am* reminding you—right now!" Jeffrey said.

But the ghost ignored Jeffrey's question. "Dig this," Max said. "We'll put a live raccoon in Robin's locker."

Jeffrey shook his head.

"Okay. We'll put a dead raccoon in his locker."

"Why don't we do whatever you did to Glasseye Willie Tufa?"

This time Max shook his head. "You don't

know what you're saying, Daddy-o," the ghost said with fear in his voice.

"Of course I don't—because you won't tell me what happened!" Jeffrey said angrily.

"Stay cool, Daddy-o. I've got it! The perfect way to make Robin Dessart's mop flop. A surprise quiz."

"You've got to be kidding, Max," Jeffrey said. "I told you, he knows *everything*. He's probably great at quizzes."

The ghost just smiled. "Like, not one of *my* quizzes," he said.

"Well, you could be right," Jeffrey said thoughtfully. "Robin is new to our class. He can't possibly know everything Mrs. Merrin will put on the quiz."

"You just make sure Mrs. Merrin gives the class a quiz. And I'll make sure Robin's answers are all totally from wrongsville," Max promised.

"I think I should warn you, Max. This plan may not work."

"Not work? Daddy-o, you bruise me the most. It's one of *my* plans!"

"I know," Jeffrey said as the ghost vanished. "And that's what's got me worried."

Chapter Four

"Good morning, Mrs. Merrin," Jeffrey said as he opened the classroom door.

"Jeffrey," she said. It came out like an expression of surprise, a question, and a greeting all rolled into one. "What are you doing at school so early?"

"Well, I just wanted to be the first person to say good morning to you, Mrs. Merrin," Jeffrey told her. He gave her a broad smile.

"Thanks," his teacher said.

Jeffrey took his seat and sat there quietly.

On Mrs. Merrin's desk was a mirror and some makeup. She brushed something on her cheeks, put on lipstick, and combed her blond hair. It was cut short again, the way it had been in the fall. "I know what you're thinking," Mrs. Merrin said.

I hope not, Jeffrey thought to himself. Because he was thinking about the great trick he and Max were going to pull on Robin Dessart: the surprise quiz!

"You're thinking, Why doesn't she do this before she comes to school, aren't you?" the teacher said with a laugh. "Because of my dog," was her answer. "My puppy has grown into an uncontrollable face licker, especially in the morning. My husband and I can't stop him." The teacher put away her makeup. "But back to square one. Why are you really here so early, Jeffrey? It's not like you."

"Mrs. Merrin, how would you like to do me a favor?"

"I don't know, Jeffrey. I consider myself a generous sweetheart by nature. But the last time you asked me, the favor was to sign a note that said you were really a midget so that you could get into an R-rated movie. What's the favor this time?"

"I'd like you to give the class a surprise quiz."

Mrs. Merrin tried to act calm. "Excuse me for double-checking, Jeffrey, but did you just say you want a quiz?"

Jeffrey nodded.

"Aren't you the same Jeffrey Becker who once told me that your ears were allergic to words that begin with the letter q—for example, quiz, question, and quiet?"

"Yeah, but I only get that allergy in the winter. Now it's spring. So how about giving us a quiz today?"

"Sounds like a good idea to me," Mrs. Merrin said.

But it didn't sound like a good idea to the rest of the class when Mrs. Merrin announced it was quiz time. There were many complaints.

You guys won't complain about it when Robin Dessart looks like a total bozo, Jeffrey thought.

Jeffrey looked over at Robin Dessart's desk. Robin hadn't come in yet. But Max was sitting at Robin's desk. Of course, he was invisible to everyone except Jeffrey and Kenny. The ghost just shrugged.

"Mrs. Merrin," Jeffrey said, raising his hand as he spoke. "The whole class isn't here yet. What about Robin? I know he'll be really disappointed if you give us a quiz without him."

"I forgot to tell you," Mrs. Merrin said. "Robin's mother called me early this morning. He won't be in class for a week or so. He has the chicken pox."

Robin, not in class? Jeffrey thought. Then who needs the quiz!

"So take out paper and pencil for our quiz," Mrs. Merrin told them.

"Quiz?" Jeffrey immediately put his head on his desk and began to moan as if he were in a lot of pain.

"What's wrong, Jeffrey?" asked Mrs. Merrin.

He held his ears tightly. "I think my *q* allergy is acting up again, Mrs. Merrin. You'd better cancel the quiz."

"But, Jeffrey, you said—"

Yikes! She was going to tell everyone that the quiz was *his* idea! Jeffrey moaned even louder to drown her out. "I need a drink of water. I'll be right back." Jeffrey started toward Max and pointed to the door with a movement of his head.

As soon as the two of them were out in the hall, Jeffrey started yelling—quietly—at the ghost. "Great plan, Max! Now we're having a quiz, thanks to you. I'll probably get so many things wrong on it that I'll get a negative score."

"No sweat, Daddy-o. Tell Mrs. Merrin you forgot how to hold a pencil," the ghost said confidently.

"I've done that. There's no way it'll work a third time," Jeffrey said. "I thought we were supposed to be teaching Robin Dessart a lesson—not me!"

"Daddy-o, even Glass-eye Willie Tufa didn't learn his lesson on the first merry-go-round. See you later, alligator."

As usual, the ghost disappeared before Jeffrey was through talking to him. A minute later, Mrs. Merrin came out into the hall looking for Jeffrey.

"Jeffrey, maybe this will help your *q* allergy.

Don't think of this as a quiz. Think of it as a *test*," said Mrs. Merrin with a smile. "Now come back into the classroom. We're waiting."

Jeffrey hobbled toward the door.

"Jeffrey, what's wrong with your leg? Why are you limping?"

"*T* words, Mrs. Merrin. They do it to me every time."

At lunch that day, Ben, Jeffrey, Melissa, Ricky, and Kenny sat together in the cafeteria.

"Whoever heard of getting the chicken pox in the third grade?" Ben asked.

Everyone at the table clucked like chickens and laughed.

"I had it in kindergarten," Kenny said.

"We all had it in kindergarten because we gave it to each other," Melissa said.

The chickens at the table started to cluck again.

"Except me," Jeffrey reminded them.

"That's right," Ben said. "You haven't had it at all."

"And I'm not going to, either," Jeffrey said. "I'm going to be the first kid in the Northern Hemisphere never to get the chicken pox. Now, do you want to hear what I've got planned for my birthday party? It's only a couple of weeks away."

Ben laughed. "The last I heard, your parents were denying that you were ever born. Therefore, you can't have a birthday party."

"They only said that because they were getting a little tired of me changing my mind about what kind of party I want," Jeffrey explained. "But I told them, 'Guys, how many times does a guy turn nine?' "

"Only once, unless you get caught in a time warp," Ben said.

"What are the choices for your party?" Melissa asked.

"The choices fall into two categories: things I want to do and things my parents will pay for," Jeffrey explained. "In the first category we have things like renting a 737 jet and taking all of us to Disney World. Or renting Yankee Stadium for an afternoon and challenging the Little League Tigers to a grudge-match game. And of course we'd win. Melissa would pitch a no-hitter."

"Now you're really going off the deep end," Ricky said.

Melissa flipped a blob of jelly at Ricky with a flick of her thumb.

"In category two, my parents are willing to

take us somewhere," Jeffrey said. "Like to a swimming pool, a movie, a baseball game, or on a camping trip for a whole weekend."

"That's really nice of them," said Kenny.

"Nice? They're just trying to protect their house," said Melissa. "Last year Ben and his special laser birthday candles almost burned the Beckers' house to a crisp."

Ben was only half listening to Melissa. He was busy working out a mathematical problem on his calculator-watch. He rechecked his figures when his first answer made him frown.

"What's wrong, Ben?" asked Jeffrey.

"Bad news, Jeffrey. Your party is in two weeks, right?" Ben asked.

"Two weeks, one day, and seven hours," Jeffrey said.

"According to my calculations," Ben continued, "and considering that the incubation period of chicken pox is approximately fourteen days, I'd say you were going to break out in spots right before your party."

"No way," Jeffrey said firmly.

The chickens clucked again.

"Hey! Now I know what to get you for your birthday," Ricky joked. "Scratch-and-sniff toys!"

Chapter Five

During the next few days, Jeffrey couldn't make a move without everyone watching and staring at him. They were all waiting for the chicken pox to appear.

"I don't see any feathers yet," Jenny Arthur said every day. "Good luck."

"Of course you'll get them," Brian Carr said between laughs. "You're the biggest chicken in the third grade."

"Thanks, Brian," Jeffrey said. "I think it's really lucky that your shoe size and your I.Q. are the same. That way you only have to remember one number."

But when Jeffrey was by himself, he said out loud, "I'm not going to get the chicken pox. For one thing, I didn't get them when everyone else did. That proves that I'm too tough for the germs. And Robin Dessart is taller than I am. So the germs probably went right over my head and missed me. And on top of that, I can't get the chicken pox for my birthday. They're not on the U.S. government list of approved birthday presents."

So far, positive thinking was working. The chicken pox hadn't appeared. But as Ben kept pointing out, the incubation period for chicken pox was eleven to fourteen days. That meant it would be a while before the spots showed up.

Meanwhile, Jeffrey's biggest problem was the fact that he couldn't decide, once and for all, what kind of birthday party to have. One day a piñata party sounded great. But by the next day he wanted a sports party—until he realized that Melissa and Ricky would win all of the events. He'd probably spend his entire party handing out awards to his two friends.

The party ideas were like clouds on a windy day. At first they looked like something, but then they quickly changed shape.

At breakfast, ten days before the party, Jeffrey sat looking into his cereal bowl. "I can't decide—"

"Jeffrey," his mother interrupted, "if you start talking about your birthday party again, I'm going to scream."

"Relax, Mom. I'm only trying to decide what to have on my cereal. Peaches or strawberries. That's all."

"Sorry," said Mrs. Becker. "I know you're having a tough time choosing a theme for your party. Maybe you're trying too hard."

"Mom, this is the most important decision of my life. It's got to be right. A bad birthday party at this stage of my life could cause permanent damage. What do you think about a tattoo party?"

"Jeffrey, I'm warning you. I'm really going to scream."

"Okay. Here's a serious idea. How about a skating party? Lots of people have skating parties, but I could pick my own music and it would be different," Jeffrey said, getting excited. "And we could set up relay races on the ice. And we'd serve snow cones for snacks and stuff like that. It's great, don't you think, Mom?"

"I think you've got to decide for yourself," Mrs. Becker said. "But if you want to check out the skating rink this afternoon, I'll drive you over to the mall."

"Thanks, Mom. I know this is going to be it."

Later that day, Jeffrey and his mother stood amid the bleachers that surrounded the large ice rink that was open all year round. A skating waltz was playing on the PA system, but not many people were skating.

"Skating's not very popular in May," Mrs. Becker said.

"That's what's cool about it, Mom," Jeffrey said. "It's great. It's cool. But is it perfect?" He rested his foot on the railing of the rink and re-tied his shoe. "Let's go skating, Mom."

"Jeffrey, I haven't skated since before you were born," Mrs. Becker said with a laugh.

"Mom, right now I'm ninety-five percent sure this is the best party idea."

"Well, if seeing me fall down on the ice is the other five percent, I'll give it a try."

They rented skates and went out on the ice. Jeffrey's legs were like pretzels for the first few minutes. But, to Jeffrey's surprise, his mother glided across the ice without a slip.

"Mom! You're great. I never knew you could skate," Jeffrey said, catching up with his mother.

She skated backward and laughed. "Your fa-ther and I used to skate all the time. I was afraid I'd forgotten how," she called back to him.

They skated around and around the rink. The waltz music blared and the lights blinked oc-

casionally. For an hour, they raced each other
and tried to skate figure eights. Then they
traded their skates for their sneakers and walked
to the car.

"Well, skating was great. But the skating party

is definitely out," Jeffrey said, buckling his seat belt.

Instead of starting the car, Mrs. Becker glared at her son. "Why?" she demanded to know.

"Mom, you're such a fabulous skater. Everyone will think the skating party was your idea and you forced me into it," Jeffrey explained. "That's too embarrassing."

Jeffrey's next party idea came to him just three days before his birthday. He rushed to tell his father, who was working at his desk in the den. "A movie party," Jeffrey said. "It's so obvious, why didn't I think of it before?"

"You did think of it before. About two weeks ago," Mr. Becker replied.

"Ideas, like fruit, have to ripen, Dad."

Mr. Becker kept studying his work. It was a blueprint of the new building at his construction site. "Well, a movie party sounds fine to me. We'll take everyone to a movie on your birthday."

"You make it sound so simple, Dad."

"It *is* simple. There are three stages: Your friends all come here. We put them into our cars. We take them to a movie."

"What if they don't like the movie?" Jeffrey

asked. "I mean, if I plan a whole party around going to a movie and everyone hates the movie, then the whole party goes right down the tubes. Glub. Glub."

Mr. Becker pushed aside his blueprint and opened up the newspaper to the movie section. "No problem. We'll just pick a movie everyone wants to see."

"Dad, when's the last time you and I agreed about a movie?"

"Nineteen seventy-two," Mr. Becker said.

"I wasn't born then," Jeffrey said.

"I know, and you were a lot easier to get along with back then. You didn't worry so much about your birthday parties. Pick a movie."

Jeffrey pointed to an ad for a new comedy called *My Summer Vacation*. "It's supposed to be funny, but I don't know if everyone will like it," Jeffrey said.

"Well, let's go check it out," his father said, smiling.

Jeffrey and his parents rushed to the movie theater just in time for the five o'clock show. During the movie they ate hot dogs for dinner and laughed so hard at the film that their popcorn went flying out of the boxes.

When they got home, Mr. Becker said, "Okay. The movie is a riot, and the movie party is a go for your birthday."

"Yeah, it's a great movie and everyone will love it," Jeffrey said. "Everyone except me."

"What's wrong?" asked Mr. Becker.

"I've already seen it," Jeffrey said.

"Jeffrey Allen Becker," Mrs. Becker announced, slamming the back door. "I want you to tell me right this minute what kind of birthday party you want!"

"You're really putting me on the spot, Mom," Jeffrey said.

Mrs. Becker rolled her eyes. "I'm your mother, Jeffrey. If I can't put you on the spot, who can?"

"Sometimes when you're angry you don't make sense, Mom."

"I'm not angry. I'm *livid*!" Mrs. Becker said. "Decide, Jeffrey. Do everyone a favor, especially yourself."

Jeffrey paced around the kitchen. Finally he said, "Okay, Mom."

"What's it going to be?" his mother asked wearily. "The pool party? The ice cream party? The goofy-hair party? The movie party?"

"I thought the tonsillectomy party had real potential," Mr. Becker said.

"That was a joke, Dad," Jeffrey said, still pacing.

"Well, how about the baseball party or the muscle-shirt party?" asked Mr. Becker.

"Okay, I've decided," Jeffrey said.

"Good," said his mother. "Which is it?"

"It's none of those," Jeffrey said.

Jeffrey's parents stepped closer to him. Their eyes were big and their mouths were open wide.

"I want to go to the Big Adventure Amusement Park. We'll go on the rides and see the animals. . . ." Jeffrey stopped talking and stared back at his parents. "What are you guys staring at? That's my decision—my final decision. Honest."

Mrs. Becker pulled Jeffrey closer.

"Say something," Jeffrey said.

"Jeffrey," Mrs. Becker said, "you have spots on your face."

Mr. Becker nodded. "You'd better forget about any party for a while. I think you've got the chicken pox."

Chapter Six

The chicken pox? Three days before his birthday? Jeffrey couldn't believe what his parents were saying. He ran to his room and locked himself inside. He didn't want to see anyone, and he didn't want anyone to see him. "I look like a pepperoni pizza," he had told Ben on the phone.

"Jeffrey, it's your mother," said Mrs. Becker, after knocking on the locked door.

"Mom, I have the chicken pox, not amnesia," Jeffrey told her.

"You're not scratching, are you?" she said.

"Every minute, Mom," Jeffrey said glumly. "I've got three back scratchers all going at once. And I'm using a sheet of sandpaper on my face."

"Jeffrey, don't upset me," said Mrs. Becker.

"I've only begun to scratch the surface," Jeffrey answered.

By the next day, Jeffrey didn't feel like making jokes about scratching. His chicken-pox

spots were everywhere: on his face, his arms,
his legs, his chest, his back, even in between
his fingers. And every single itchy one seemed
to say, "Go ahead. Scratch me."

His mother dabbed calamine lotion on him and Jeffrey felt like a turkey being basted.

"Couldn't you just load up a paint sprayer with the stuff, Mom? Or—I've got it!—how about lowering me into a huge vat of it. I could wear scuba equipment and just stay under until it's over."

His mother smiled. "At least the chicken pox hasn't affected your imagination."

"Mom, things are tough enough without you looking on the bright side of everything," Jeffrey said. Then he added, "Just two more days till my birthday."

"But it's eight more days till you're all better," she replied.

Eight days until he was better . . . So what? By the time Jeffrey was itch-free, his birthday would have come and gone and no one would have noticed.

Jeffrey's birthday came two days later—along with more red spots. That day, Jeffrey made a law in his house against anyone using the *b* word. After that, he just lay in bed all morning, thinking of ways to keep from scratching. He was just about to try the PJ challenge—changing his pajamas without using his hands or feet—when his bedroom door opened with a bang.

At first Jeffrey stared at his visitor as though she were from outer space. "Melissa!" He was so happy to see her, he shouted her name.

"Hi, Jeffrey," Melissa said cheerfully. "How's it going?"

"Oh, terrific," Jeffrey said. "I think I can finally beat you at something. I have more chicken-pox spots than you have freckles. What are you doing here, anyway?"

"Your dad just called and told me to come over right away," Melissa said, sitting down on Jeffrey's bed.

"No, he didn't. I told him I didn't want to see anyone. And besides, my dad isn't even home," Jeffrey insisted.

"Jeffrey Becker, I don't lie," Melissa said.

"Is someone arguing? I love arguing," said Ben, as he walked into the room. Kenny was close behind him. "What's the argument?" Ben asked. "Whatever it is, I'm on Jeffrey's side."

"Hi, Jeffrey," said Kenny. "Happy—" Kenny stopped himself just before he broke the no *b*-word law. "Uh, happy to see you," he said instead.

Melissa put her hands on her hips. "Jeffrey

doesn't believe me," she explained to Ben. "I told him that his father called to tell me to come over, but he doesn't believe it."

"Of course he did," Ben agreed. "He called me, too."

"It's true," Kenny added. "I was at Ben's house."

"Hey, you guys!" said Ricky Reyes, as he stood in the doorway. "I didn't know all of you were going to be here. What is this—a party or something?"

"Pull up a floor and sit down," Jeffrey said, happily watching his room become crowded with all of his best friends.

"Did Jeffrey's dad call you, too?" asked Ben.

"Yeah, but he sounded really weird," said Ricky. "He said if I came over for Jeffrey's birthday, it would be totally coolsville."

Jeffrey and Kenny looked at each other quickly. Coolsville? That didn't sound like Mr. Becker. It could only be Max.

Suddenly, each of the window shades lowered, one after the other. And all the lights in the room went out—by themselves.

"Great trick," Melissa said calmly. "How did you do it, Ben?"

"Me? Don't ask me," said Ben, not as calmly.

Ricky tried the light switch by the open door. The lights came on, but then went out again. "It's broken or something," he reported. All of a sudden, Ricky started backing away from the door—fast. His eyes were glued on something in the hallway. "You guys! Get back. Get out of the way!"

The five friends stood back and stared at the doorway. Something was coming. Something weird—something so weird that even Ricky Reyes sounded nervous. What could it be? Everyone held their breath.

It was a large, three-layer birthday cake floating into the room—*all by itself*. It had thick white icing and lots of red polka dots that looked a lot like chicken-pox spots.

"I don't see any strings," Melissa said. "And I don't see anyone carrying it." She sounded nervous and surprised.

Jeffrey, of course, saw who was carrying the cake. And so did Kenny. It was Max. He was even showing off, balancing the cake on his head and walking into the room with his arms behind his back.

"Hey, Daddy-o's," Max said, looking at Jeffrey and Kenny. "Tell these cats to close their mouths. If they think I'm going to feed them, they'd better hop a bus back to dreamsville."

"Jeffrey, how are you doing that?" Ben asked, staring at the moving cake.

"Uh, it's angel food cake," Jeffrey said. "Angels can fly, you know."

The sight of a birthday cake floating into the room amazed Jeffrey's friends. But when, one by one, the cake's candles began to light themselves, Melissa, Ben, and Ricky totally freaked out. They couldn't move. They couldn't talk. They just stared, frozen and silent.

Max stared right back at them. "Why don't they take a picture?" he joked.

Kenny broke the silence by singing "Happy Birthday" to Jeffrey. And soon everyone joined in, including Max.

When the song was over, Ben said softly, "Jeffrey, I'll do anything—anything you want—if you tell me how you're doing this trick."

"Chill out. I'm going to make a wish and blow out the candles," Jeffrey said. It didn't take him any time to think of his wish. It was the same one he had been wishing every since September when he first met Max. He wanted *all* of his friends to be able to see the ghost.

It took just one strong breath to blow out all the candles. And then Jeffrey watched as Max sliced the cake. Melissa, Ben, and Ricky still thought that a knife was flying through the air and cutting pieces of cake all by itself. But Jeffrey and Kenny knew better. Then Max served the cake to everyone, leaving the biggest slice for himself.

"Jeffrey," said Melissa in a shaky voice, "what's going on? Is this really happening or have I seen too many freaky ghost movies?"

"Like, watch who you're calling freaky," Max said.

Melissa's head jerked around. "Who said that?" she asked.

Jeffrey almost dropped his plate. "Melissa! You mean you heard that?"

"Of course I heard that," Melissa said.

Ben and Ricky had heard it, too.

"Jeffrey, that was you talking, wasn't it?" Ben asked slowly.

Just then Max started to fly around the room. "Ready or not," he said, "like, here I make the scene!"

Melissa, Ben, and Ricky practically jumped out of their shoes and socks when they saw first the hands, then the feet, then the entire third-grade ghost. Max was making himself visible to them!

"What is that?" Melissa said. Even her freckles looked pale.

Jeffrey was so happy that he was nearly flying himself. His wish had come true. "You can see him?"

"Yes!" Ben shouted, ducking down as Max swooped over him. "What is it?"

"It's Max. It's the ghost I've been telling you about since the beginning of school!" Jeffrey shouted, smiling at Max.

The ghost smiled back. "Like, Happy Birthday the most, Jeffrey," he said.

Chapter Seven

Max was too excited to come down from the ceiling. He had never made himself visible to so many people at once. It was a gas! He floated around the room over everyone's heads.

"No. No. No," Ben moaned. "This isn't scientific. It isn't really happening."

"Yes, it is, Ben. It's finally *really* happening," Jeffrey told him. "I've been wanting you guys to meet Max all year."

"I still don't believe it," Ricky said.

"You don't believe Max exists?" Jeffrey asked.

"I believe that—no problem," Ricky said with a grin. "What I can't believe is that you were really telling the truth about something, Jeffrey."

Meanwhile, Melissa tried to grab the ghost from behind. Of course, her hands passed right through him. "But he looks as real as we do," she said.

Max rolled his eyes and laughed. "As you cats today say, cut me a break, will ya?" he said. " 'Let's grab the ghost'—that trick is so oldsville it creaks. Watch this."

With a superfast swing, Max punched Melissa right in the stomach. She flinched, but she didn't have to. Max's hand went right through her and she didn't feel a thing.

For the rest of that afternoon, Jeffrey lay in bed. His four old friends, and their new friend Max, sat on the rug. They talked and laughed about all the weird things that had happened during the school year. Things that Melissa, Ben, Kenny, and Ricky hadn't understood before. Now they knew that those things had happened because of Max.

"What about the time you and I went into the creepy old McGyver house on Halloween?" asked Ben. "Weren't you really scared?"

"Sure," Jeffrey said. "But Max was helping us all the way. And remember when Mrs. Merrin lost her wallet on a field trip? Who do you think found it?"

"Like, I'm blushing already, Daddy-o," Max said.

"Gee," Melissa said, "during my ballet recital, when I was standing on pointe, I thought

I was going to fall over. Then suddenly it felt like someone was holding me up. Was that you, Max?"

"Lucky for you, I dig dancing the most," said the ghost. "Like, I wrote *Duck Lake* all by myself."

"Max, the ballet is called *Swan Lake*," Melissa said.

"Uh, well, mine is different," the ghost replied.

"Hey, how about the time Arvin Pubbler tripped in the lunch line and spilled two trays of chocolate pudding all over himself?" asked Ben. "Did you do that, Max?"

The ghost shook his head. "Daddy-o, that cat doesn't need any help from me in the clumsy department."

Ben cleared his throat, something he usually did just before asking one of his scientific questions. "Max, what does it feel like to be . . ." Ben stopped. He could see that Max's expression was getting serious. "To be not entirely alive," Ben said.

Max thought about it for a few seconds, stretching a long string of bubble gum out of his mouth and putting it back. "Well, Daddy-o, I'm going to give you the whole-truth-and-nothing-but-the-truth answer to that question. So hold on tight," he said. "You know that feeling you get when you, like, eat ice cream too fast?"

"Sure," Ben answered, sitting up excitedly. "It feels like your nose is going to fall off. I know exactly how that feels."

"Well, it's nothing like that," Max said, then burst out laughing.

Jeffrey leaned over his bed to tell Ben, "Rule number one with Max: Never ask a straight question. That way you won't be disappointed when you don't get a straight answer."

"Okay, cats, now it's time to empty your pockets," Max said seriously. He looked straight at Ben, Melissa, and Ricky.

"Why?" Melissa asked. "I don't have any money with me, anyway."

Jeffrey frowned. "What is this, Max? A holdup?"

"Daddy-o, sometimes you're a real ice cube— you're cool but you're square," said the ghost.

Finally, Jeffrey's friends did what Max said. They emptied their pockets onto the rug. Then Max looked at everyone's pile of stuff and took one thing from each pile. From Ben he took a key ring with a small solar cell. From Ricky he took a small, hard rubber ball that Ricky squeezed to strengthen his hand muscles. And from Melissa he took a comb. The ghost put the three things in his right jeans pocket.

Then he took something out of his left pocket: two old steel nails, twisted loosely and bent together. "Daddy-o, are you smart enough to beat my record for getting them apart?" Max asked, handing Ben the puzzle. Ben pulled and twisted and got it apart in thirty seconds. Max smiled.

Then Max gave Ricky a collapsible plastic drinking mug. Printed on the mug's removable cap was a face that looked like somebody's dad's. But Max insisted the guy was the coolest superhero in the world—in the 1950s.

And finally he gave Melissa five Elvis Presley records.

"Wow!" Melissa said, flipping through them. "Fabulous oldies!"

"Oldies?" said Max. "Like, those are my newest platters."

"I mean, thanks, Max," Melissa said.

"Well, now, you guys, it's official!" said the ghost. "Like, it's friendsville for us forever."

During the next week, even though Jeffrey was getting over the chicken pox, he still had to stay home. His friends spent their days in school, but afterwards they'd race to Jeffrey's house to keep him company. There was lots of news to tell, and, besides, they also wanted to be with Max.

"Hey, you know who was back in school?" asked Kenny. "Robin Dessart."

"Don't talk about him while I'm eating, okay?" joked Ricky, who was chomping on some vanilla-cream sandwich cookies.

"You'll be back in school soon, too, Jeffrey," said Kenny.

"Yeah, I'll be back," Jeffrey said. "That's why I've got to think of a way to get even with Robin Dessart for giving me the chicken pox."

This made Max laugh.

"What's so funny?" Jeffrey asked the ghost.

"Daddy-o, it's like looking in a mirror and seeing me say the same thing about Glass-eye Willie Tufa."

"Who's that?" asked Kenny.

"That's a kid Max knew," Jeffrey explained. "Max says he was ten times more obnoxious than Robin Dessart."

"Fifty times," said the ghost.

"That's not what you said," Jeffrey argued.

"Well, I got my first good look at this cat, Robin, today. He's a bowl of soggy cereal compared to Glass-eye Willie."

"What happened between you two?" Ricky asked.

"They got into a fight," Jeffrey said.

"Daddy-o, like, I never said me and the Glass-eye got into a fight. It was nothing like that," Max said.

"Well, what *did* happen?" Kenny asked.

"Hey, wait a minute," Jeffrey said. He was getting an idea, so he reached down to retie his shoe.

"Forget it, Jeffrey," said Ben. "You're wearing your bedroom slippers."

"But what's your idea?" asked Melissa.

"I'm going to invite Robin Dessart to my be-
lated birthday party at Big Adventure," Jeffrey
said with a gleam in his eyes.

"That's not my idea of a good time," Ricky
said.

"It *will* be when you think of all the things
Max could do to Robin," Jeffrey said.

"I've got it!" Kenny said. "You mean, Max
could put an ice cream sandwich on Robin's seat
right before he sits down on a ride."

"Too wimpy," Melissa said.

"True. Kenny, you'd better leave the mean
stuff to us," Jeffrey told him.

"How about this?" asked Ben. "Max could
really, *really* scare Robin in the haunted house.
He's certainly qualified to do it."

"Hey, like, cool it, Daddy-o's," Max said.
"What if yours truly doesn't want to make that
scene?"

"You've *got* to help us, Max," Melissa said.

"What about friendsville forever?" asked
Ben.

"No one can do tricks the way you can," said
Kenny.

"And you can do the same thing you did to
Glass-eye Willie Tufa," Jeffrey said.

"Now you're sending and I'm receiving,

Daddy-o," said the ghost with a smile. "That would be a gas!"

"So tell us: *What did you do to Glass-eye Willie Tufa?*" Jeffrey, Kenny, Ben, Melissa, and Ricky all asked at the same time.

"See you later, alligators," said the ghost, disappearing instantly.

"Isn't he ever going to tell us?" Ben asked.

"Max lives in his own time zone," Jeffrey said. "But when I finally have my birthday party, I bet we'll find out!"

Chapter Eight

On the day of the birthday-party trip to Big Adventure Amusement Park, Jeffrey was the birthday boy. But the way Jeffrey planned it, Robin Dessart was the guest of honor. When the doorbell rang, Jeffrey and friends burst out laughing.

"Very unusual response to the doorbell," remarked Mr. Becker. "Most people just open the door. What's going on, Jeffrey?"

"We were just telling ghost stories, Dad," Jeffrey said on his way to the door. He opened the door with an enthusiastic "Hi."

Robin almost stepped back, he was so surprised by Jeffrey's friendliness. "Hi," he said, handing Jeffrey a birthday present and shaking his hand formally.

"Thanks," Jeffrey said. He gave the package to his mother, who was standing nearby. "Call the bomb squad," he told her quietly as he led Robin into the living room. "Hey, you guys," Jeffrey called. "Robin's here."

Melissa, Ben, Kenny, and Ricky looked at Robin and then laughed again.

"The fun's going to start now," Ricky said.

"I get it. You didn't want me to come," said Robin.

"N.T.," said Jeffrey. "Not true. In fact, this party would be a total flop without you."

They went in two cars. Mrs. Becker drove Kenny, Melissa, and Ricky. Mr. Becker drove Jeffrey, Robin, and Ben. Even though Mr. Becker's car was small, there was room for more people. But Jeffrey insisted that one seat be left empty—for Max.

But was Max sitting there? Was he keeping himself invisible even to Jeffrey? Or had he forgotten about the party entirely?

There was no way to know until they got to the Maniac Mudslide, the first ride they were going to try.

"You go first," Jeffrey told Robin.

"It's your birthday," Robin said, looking up toward the top of the long and winding slide.

"Hey, it's cinchy," Jeffrey said. "You sit on one of those rug things and you sort of steer yourself down the slide."

"Of course," added Ben, "if you steer the

wrong way, you go flying into those deep, thick mud holes along the sides."

"I understand the principle of the ride," Robin said. "And if you guys want me to go first to show you how it's done, I can handle that."

Robin climbed to the top of the slide.

"When do you think Max is going to push him into the mud?" asked Melissa.

"The question isn't when but how many times," Jeffrey said, and they all laughed.

They watched as Robin zipped down the Maniac Mudslide. He went twisting around the sharp curves and speeding down the narrow straightaways. He screamed all the way, just like every other kid on the ride. But Max didn't push him into the mud.

Robin stepped off the slide as clean as when he got on, and with a big smile.

"What's next?" he asked the rest of the group.

"Let's go on to the Hullaballoo," Jeffrey said impatiently. "Maybe we might even meet someone we know there."

Jeffrey, Ben, and Kenny quickly climbed into the first car of the Hullaballoo, and Melissa and Ricky got into a car with another kid. That left

Robin to ride in a car by himself. So far the plan was working out.

The second part of the plan was Max's job. He was supposed to guide two little kids into Robin's car. These kids would be eating hot dogs with lots of mustard or licking soft ice cream cones or drinking giant sodas. Then when the ride started, Max would squeeze into the car, too. As soon as the ride started spinning, Max would "help" the kids spill food all over Robin.

Robin was supposed to come out looking as if he just stepped out of a milkshake machine.

When the ride slowed down, Jeffrey and his friends ran out of their cars to watch Robin.

"Look at him. I don't believe it," Melissa said.

"There's not a spot on him," said Ricky.

Ben watched for a moment more and said, "That's because no one else was in the car with him."

"Max isn't here," Kenny said.

"He's here," Jeffrey told them. "He's just saving it all for the grand finale. Just remember Glass-eye Willie Tufa."

"Wow," Robin said, running up to them. "I've got to admit, this is a terrific park. And I've been to the best of them. Hey, let's find some food."

Food. Sure, Jeffrey thought. What was Max going to try at the refreshment stand? The old loosen-the-cap-on-the-mustard-squirter trick? Flies stuck in Robin's cotton candy? Or maybe show-off Robin would offer to pay for the food and Max would hide his wallet.

But nothing like that happened to Robin at all. In fact, Robin told a joke that made Melissa laugh so hard that soda went up her nose. And that just made everyone laugh harder.

"Well, great," grumbled Ben. "Thanks to Max, this plan is totally falling apart."

"Yeah," Jeffrey muttered.

"There's the Harem Scare'em Cars," Kenny said. "They're like dodge-'em cars except they don't have any steering wheels."

"You can ride with me," Melissa told Robin.

Jeffrey was going to jump into his favorite red car, but he felt an invisible hand holding him back. "You guys go on," he said. "I want to watch."

As soon as the ride began, Max made himself visible to Jeffrey. The two friends leaned on the wood railing and watched the cars skid and bump into one another like crazy.

"Where've you been, Max?" Jeffrey asked.

"I've been doing what you asked me to do, Daddy-o," said Max.

"Max, you haven't done any of the tricks we told you to do," Jeffrey said.

"But, Daddy-o, both of my ears heard you tell me to do the same thing to Robin that I did to old Glass-eye Willie Tufa. Am I lying or flying?"

"Right, and I've been waiting all afternoon," Jeffrey said. "What *did* you do to that kid? Fight him? Sue him? Dip him in a tub of lard? I give up!"

"No, Daddy-o, that's all strictly squaresville. Like, this is what I did with the Glass-eye—I made friends with him," Max replied. "I gave him half a chance, and deep insidesville, he was a pretty cool cat. Not as cool as you, Jeffrey, but he and I got to be tight as a Band-Aid and a boo-boo."

Jeffrey turned away from the ghost. "You tricked me, Max. I thought you were going to dog Robin and ruin his day at my party."

"I can still make with the mean scene if that's what you really want," the ghost offered.

Jeffrey thought about Robin and how he was trying to be nicer, almost human. Then he thought about giving Robin half a chance and about what might happen.

"You still want me to flip Robin out?" Max asked.

Jeffrey shook his head. "Hey, if it worked with Glass-eye Willie Tufa, maybe it'll work for me," he said.

Jeffrey ran to catch up with his other friends. He hurried past the ring toss, the basketball toss, and a strange new game called the salad toss. When he found his friends, they were standing in front of the balloon dart game.

Robin came up to Jeffrey. "This is a superior

party in every way, Jeffrey," he said. "I know I'm not the easiest guy to understand . . . I mean, to like. That's why I'm really glad you invited me." Robin gave an embarrassed shrug. "And from now on I'm going to try not to act like such a know-it-all."

Jeffrey smiled. "Yeah, well, I figured it's always rough to move to a new city. You probably had to leave all your friends behind, too."

"Yeah," Robin admitted. "And I didn't have any choice. My mother and father just got a divorce."

"That's a real bummer," Ricky Reyes said, and he sounded really sorry.

Jeffrey and his friends looked at each other. The look said: Okay, let's cut this guy a break.

"Hey, Robin, I'll bet you're pretty good at darts," Melissa said in her friendliest voice.

"Pretty good is a complete understatement, of course," Robin said. He led the way to the balloon dart game and spent about two minutes picking out the best darts. "Getting the right weight is crucial," he explained. Then he threw six darts and burst five balloons. "I can show you my technique sometime if you guys want," he added, as he claimed the second biggest prize—a giant green stuffed lizard.

"He's going to have to try a lot harder not to be such a know-it-all," Ben mumbled in Jeffrey's ear.

"No kidding," Jeffrey agreed. "I wish Max could see Robin now."

But it was Ricky's turn with the darts, so Jeffrey forgot about Max for a minute. Then one by one Ben, Melissa, and Kenny each took a turn with the darts. To Robin's surprise, *all* of them hit five balloons with six tries and each won a giant green stuffed lizard.

For a minute Jeffrey was really surprised, too. But then suddenly Max appeared, standing by the wall of balloons with a pin in his hand.

"Come on, Daddy-o," called Max. "You can't miss. Same as the others. You've got my personal guarantee."

Jeffrey grinned. He threw five darts and Max popped five balloons, even when Jeffrey's darts were way off the mark. Then finally there was only one dart to go. Could Jeffrey do better than everyone else? Jeffrey closed his eyes and threw.

The crowd gasped and Jeffrey opened his eyes quickly. Max had popped *two* balloons that time! Jeffrey had gotten *seven* balloons with only *six* darts! The balloon man shook his head in amazement, but he handed Jeffrey the best prize—a giant stuffed monster holding a baby gorilla.

"Gifted throwing, you guys," Robin said. "You certainly don't need any tips from me."

"We've been taking lessons," Jeffrey said, "from a guy named Max." And his friends smiled.

"I've got to meet him sometime," Robin said as they walked away from the dart game.

"Well, he comes and goes," Kenny said quickly.

Ricky laughed. "He kind of sneaks up on you."

"Now you see him and now you don't," Melissa said.

"Unpredictable," added Ben.

"Gee, you guys make him sound like a ghost or something," Robin said.

"Not a ghost," Jeffrey said, winking at Ben. "Just a friend—a really good friend."

*Here's a peek at Jeffrey's next adventure with Max, the **fourth**-grade ghost!*

MAX IS BACK

"This is the first day of school," Jeffrey said excitedly to Max. "You know what that means, don't you? A new teacher to drive crazy. And a few days when we can get away with anything. Besides that, we're fourth graders now."

"What do you mean *we*?" the ghost said, shaking his head. "Daddy-o, like, I was in the third grade right before I took my one-way trip to ghostville and I've been there ever since. Of course, I could have gone into fourth grade anytime I wanted. But, like, who wants to? If fourth grade is so cool, then why do cats only stay there *one year*?"

"Because if we just stayed in the same classroom forever, we wouldn't fit in the desks," Jeffrey explained. "I grew exactly three and a quarter inches over the summer. And you're taller, too, Max." Jeffrey cocked his head a little to the side. He brushed his thick brown hair out of his eyes so he could see his friend better. "Max, are you scared to go into the fourth grade or something?"

"Like, forget it," Max said with a frown.

"Well then, let's go," Jeffrey said. He ran up the stairs. But when he turned around at the front door to make sure that Max was coming, Max had disappeared.

ABOUT THE AUTHORS

Bill and Megan Stine have written numerous books for young readers, including titles in these series: *The Cranberry Cousins; Wizards, Warriors, and You; The Three Investigators; Indiana Jones; G.I. Joe;* and *Jem.* They live on New York City's Upper West Side with their seven-year-old son, Cody, who believes in ghosts.